THE BOOK OF DREAMS

BY

Andrew Luna

https://www.moonwriting.me

Contents

The Book of Dreams

PROLOGUE

These stories are all drawn from the vivid

tapestries of my dreams. Yet, encapsulating these

ephemeral reveries into words posed a challenge. Upon

waking, the remnants of these tales linger in my mind, like

scattered fragments of a puzzle. My task, then, was to

painstakingly piece them together, sometimes altering

their course to fill gaps or render them coherent. The true

challenge lay in transforming these dreamscapes into

tangible stories with plots, often hindered by the hazy

recollection or enigmatic nature of dreams.
The Book of Dreams

I hope this explanation resonates with you, for sharing these dreams-turned-stories is a deeply personal endeavor. No one else will dream the exact dreams I did—though perhaps, in reading these stories, you'll find yourself immersed in my nocturnal visions. Or, perhaps, these tales will spark a new narrative in your own slumbering mind. This, indeed, is one of life's remarkable facets: the realm of dreams. While delving into the science behind dreams isn't my intent, it's worth noting that, when we dream, we're essentially authoring our own stories.

Who knows? Maybe this existence is but a grand dream, and someday we'll awaken to embark on a new journey. I extend my gratitude to you for delving into these stories, once woven from my dreams. Special thanks go to Angelica Polis for her editing prowess and to Samra Mahboob for the splendid cover design.

The Book of Dreams

STORY 1 — FIRST DAY AT THE OFFICE

"And this is where your desk is," the man said to me.

"Thank you, Carl," I said. "I am excited to get started."

Carl smiled at me. "Now don't be such an eager beaver. It

is just your first day. I don't expect you to get a lot done.

Here, meet Christopher. He will be your friend and

developer on this project."

I looked over and saw a man around my age sitting in a

similar black office chair. He wore a black sports cap,

hoodie, and glasses. He paid no attention to us and

The Book of Dreams

continued focusing on his computer monitor, which was filled with large lines of code.

"Thanks," I said as Carl walked away from me.

"Hi Christopher, my name is Andrew." I held out my hand for him to shake, but he paid no attention to my introduction. "Christopher?" I repeated.

"Huh? Oh sorry! I was focused on trying to fix this bug," he answered. "Nice to meet you, I am Chris, just call me Chris. Only my enemies and my wife call me Christopher."

"Okay, that's... fair," I replied. "So today is my first day."

"Cool man. Cool. Welcome. I guess we'll be working together, right? You're the new QA guy?"

"Yeah, that's correct. I am. How long have you been a developer?"

"Too damn long. At least twenty-something years now. I don't really know to be honest. I lost track. Let's see what year is it? Okay yeah, I started here as a contractor and

The Book of Dreams

then was promoted to Junior Dev. Now I am a Senior. That

sounds about right."

"Cool," I said. "Well, I am going to check out the rest of the

floor."

"Go for it. There's a hot chick over near where the

designers sit. I think her name is Kimberly. She is also new

like you."

"Thanks for the info," I said, feeling slightly awkward.

I walked around the floor and saw fellow

coworkers pass me by. Some were engaged in a serious

conversation while others engaged in small talk about the

weather. No one really paid any attention to the new guy,

which was both unsurprising and sad. I was hoping to

make new connections on my first day since chances were,

I would be working with the majority of everyone I passed.

"Excuse me, are you Andrew?"

The Book of Dreams

"Yes, I am," I eagerly answered the man, who was dressed in a suit. Compared to everyone else on this floor he was the only one dressed like a lawyer or manager. I assumed he was a higher-up, possibly the CEO.

"Great. I was looking for you. My name is Thomas. I am here to give you a tour, but I have to make a quick call. Can I meet you at your desk in say," he looked at his fancy silver watch. "Fifteen minutes?"

"Sure," I answered half eagerly and half nervously.

"Great, sport! See you then!"

I returned to my desk and powered on my laptop. The first day on the job always left me wondering what to expect. First days at a new job are never really planned. It is always about going with the flow. My expectations were low, but I hoped it would be a smooth day. A part of me still had the nervous first day jitters. I suppose that is better than the case of the Mondays. Although, today is

The Book of Dreams

also Monday. Perhaps I have both first day jitters and a case of the Mondays. I looked over and saw Chris knee-deep in JavaScript.

His hand was cupped under his unshaven face. His beard was a mixture of salt and pepper-colored hair. I wondered how old he was since he did look relatively young despite the beard. It gave me the impression that he was some sort of technological wizard or maybe even a former mercenary. The guy looked like he could star in his own action movie.

"Hey Andrew," he abruptly said.

"Yeah?" I nervously replied, hoping he did not notice me staring at him.

"I need your help with something."

"Sure Chris, what's up?"

"So, I am working on this new formula and I am a bit stumped."

The Book of Dreams

"A new formula?"

"Yeah," he answered with a slight chuckle. "Sorry. I am working on a project to build a new AI brain. I am calling him Chris Junior. This will be my son that will carry my legacy."

"Okay," I replied. I could not help but wonder if this was all some sort of clever ruse or if this guy was serious.

"Yeah, and I am stumped on this math problem."

"A math problem? What sort of math problem?" I asked.

"Would you happen to know what the square root of three cubed is?" He looked at me and pointed at some code on the screen. "This is where I am stumped."

"What kind of code is this? I thought this was JavaScript," I questioned.

"Yeah. Up here," he answered, pointing at his other monitor. "This right here, this is my secret project." He pointed at the monitor in front of us. "I am working on

The Book of Dreams

something big here. I am inventing a new type of AI code called Gom Code."

"Gom Code?" What does Gom stand for? Great One Machine?"

My question caused an unexpected chuckle from him. "No, it's actually part of my last name. But that's pretty funny. I like that."

"Okay, so you need to know what the square root of three cubed is."

"Exactly. Do you know?"

I shook my head. Hell, no I don't. Math was never my strong suit."

"I think there is one of those Texas Instrument calculators around here. Can you go and find one for me? Preferably a T-90X, that would probably help me."

"Sure. Wow, I haven't used one of those since my high school days," I said. "I used to play this game on there,

The Book of Dreams

called Drug Deal. I would basically sell and trade drugs in the game."

Upon hearing my remark, Chris began laughing profusely.

"Oh yeah! I remember that game! Imagine how much those prices would be now."

"Ah, there you are!" the man said from behind me. It was Thomas.

"Hi Thomas," I said while standing up.

Chris spun his chair around and refocused on his computer monitors.

"Are you ready for that tour, champ?"

I felt a slight cringe from his question but smiled unnervingly at him. "Sure, ready to go!" I remarked.

"Such an eager beaver. It's just your first day!" he added, slapping my shoulder lightly. "Come on, let me show you around. We have a lot of ground to cover."

The Book of Dreams

The company, Micro-Tech Industries, took up four floors of the building. The first floor was where the salespeople, library, and main lobby were located. The second floor consisted of the marketing and PR team. The third floor was our floor, which was the technology team. Finally, the fourth floor was where the CEO and other VPs were located. The rest of the building belonged to a hospital, called We Fix You. It was a weird setup, but it made it easy and convenient to have a physical during lunch.

"So, this is the first floor," Thomas proudly said, waving his arm around. "Here is where our beloved receptionist Lydia greets all of our important clients. Hi Lydia, this is the new guy, Andrew."

"Hi Lydia," I said, introducing myself.

Lydia rudely waved at me while she was staring at her phone. She really did not care or want to be bothered.

The Book of Dreams

In fact, the only enthusiastic person in the room was

Thomas, who was full-on cringe. His energy was a bit much

to handle on a Monday at ten in the morning.

"Okay, follow me," continued Thomas. Next, we entered a

large office space containing numerous tables and desks. A

bunch of jocular guys sat around laughing and yelling at

one another. The room smelled like a college dorm or frat

house. I expected nothing less and assumed this was the

sales team.

"Hey everyone, meet Andrew, our new QA guy!" Thomas

proudly introduced me.

"Hey Drew," one of the guys yelled from across the room. I

wanted to correct him, but I let it slide.

"Hey, welcome. Your name is what again? Dave?" one of

the salesmen asked.

"Andrew," I answered.

"Nice to meet you. I am Mike, but everyone calls me Fiesta."

"Fiesta? Why that?"

"Because I like to party. I got really hammered at our last holiday party. They found me pounding Lydia in the stairwell. We were really going at it."

I smiled nervously at Mike's remark and looked over at Thomas, who was engaged in a conversation with another guy dressed in a suit. I assumed this was the guy who was the head of sales. Together the two of us went onto the second floor, where he showed me where the marketing and PR team sat. This was rather brief since no one even noticed we were there. It was rather loud on this floor since the PR team was engaged in a heated conversation. I caught the end of it with someone calling Stacy an idiot for believing that mermaids were real. We skipped the third floor and went straight to the fourth.

The Book of Dreams

As the elevator doors opened, I was greeted by an older man in a sports jacket and blue t-shirt, which was of a band from the nineties. He was speaking to another person in a suit, but upon seeing us enter the floor, he quickly ended his conversation and approached us.

"Hey Thomas," the man greeted my guide.

"Hello Bob, this is the new QA guy."

"Hi," I cheerfully said.

"Nice to meet you, new QA guy, I am Bob."

"Nice to meet you, Bob."

"Listen Thomas, when you have time can you swing by my office? I need to talk numbers with you."

"You got it, boss!" Thomas proudly answered.

As Bob stepped away from us, Thomas looked at me and smiled.

"Well, this concludes our tour. I hope you enjoyed it as much as I did."

The Book of Dreams

"It was... interesting. Thank you, Thomas."

"No problem, champ! You will be great here!"

"By the way," I said. "Do you know where I can find a calculator? I mean not just any calculator, but a Texas Instrument. Preferably a T-90X?"

"Ah, the T-90X! I remember using one in middle school. Me and the gents would see who could solve math problems the quickest on it. Those were the days!"

Thomas lightly slapped my shoulder. "Check the library. I believe they will have everything that you need."

"Thank you, Thomas!"

I left the fourth floor and jumped into the elevator to travel down to the first floor. Unfortunately, the stairwell only allowed people to exit within the ground floor, which was where the parking garage was located. I entered the library and was greeted by a snobby woman who was dressed as if she were going to Sunday mass.

The Book of Dreams

"Hi, I am looking for a Texas Instrument T-90X. Is there one in stock?"

"A T-90X? Sure thing, give me a moment. Go and wait over there," the woman directed me to sit in front of a computer.

"Okay," I answered.

I sat in front of a vintage computer and monitor, which simultaneously turned on as I sat in front of it. Large green digital letters appeared on the screen welcoming me. I decided to kill some time and check out what kind of computer this was. After logging into the machine, something unexpected happened. An adult movie suddenly began playing on the screen. Luckily, the sound was muted, but it was still visibly bright for anyone passing by to notice what was happening on the screen. I had to turn my head slightly to really understand what was happening.

The Book of Dreams

"Excuse me, sir," the woman from before returned. "I

believe I have found your T-90X."

Her eyes were focused on the calculator as she

approached me. I quickly began clicking on the keyboard

and mouse, hoping to change the screen. With my eyes

focused more on the woman than what was happening on

the screen, I panicked.

"Oh, what is that?" the woman questioned. "Sir, we do not

allow that here. Please wait here."

"No wait. This was already on the screen when I sat

down!"

Despite my protests, the woman walked away from

me. I turned around and saw the movie changed to a

space movie. Somehow, in my state of panic, I managed to

change the movie to something else. Regardless, I was still

in trouble. Behind me, the elevator doors opened, and

Thomas entered the library. Seeing him was almost like

The Book of Dreams

seeing night and day because the man from earlier was no more. Instead, I was met by an angry tall, slender man. His red hair was disheveled.

"What's this I hear about you watching movies at work?"

"Oh no, it was a mistake. You see..."

"I don't want to hear it, young man. I know this is your first day and all, but we do not accept that type of behavior here. The only movies we allow are training videos."

"Well, you see when I..." I began to speak again.

"He was watching some sort of space film. Before that, I think it was some sort of sporting event. It looked like a wrestling match. I couldn't really tell because he changed it almost immediately upon seeing me," the woman interrupted.

"Why are you down here again, Andrew?" Thomas scornfully questioned me.

The Book of Dreams

I opened my mouth to speak when the woman handed the man the T-90X calculator.

"He came for this," she answered on my behalf.

"Right. The T-90."

"X," I added.

"What was that?" Thomas asked.

"Nothing."

"Come with me, young man. We need to have a talk with you."

Inside the crowded elevator, I was surrounded by several coworkers along with Bob and Thomas. It was unnervingly and unsettlingly hot inside. My body started to sweat from a mixture of anxiety and from the heat. Bob and Thomas stared at me. Thomas was quietly explaining the situation to Bob.

"He did now, did he?" Bob mumbled. "On company time?" I see. "And what do you have to say about that, Andrew?"

The Book of Dreams

I cleared my throat. "You see, sir, when I sat down, I logged into the computer and it automatically took me to a movie. I had no idea what type of movie it was or what I was truly watching, but that is what happened. But you know, at my last company, during downtime we were allowed recreation time."

"Recreation time? What's that?" Bob questioned me harshly.

I felt like I was being interrogated by a balding, stocky, and angry short detective rather than the boss of the company.

"It's when we do activities that give us time to recharge. It also helps us get through our day."

"Is that right?" Bob replied.

I could not figure out if the man was being sarcastic or genuinely honest.

"Well, that is a great idea! I would promote you if I could, but it is your first day and all. Thomas, take this man to the

The Book of Dreams

cafeteria and get him a Micro-Burger! On the house, of course! Feel free to add cheese, too. Splurge a little. Bring me one, too, we'll share a meal together."

"That's great, sir. Thank you," I replied. I wanted to mention my allergies and me being a pescatarian, but decided to just accept my Micro-Burger fate.

After we exited the elevator, I entered the fifth floor with Thomas, which is where the cafeteria was located. This was shared by both Micro-Tech and the hospital. There were a number of hospital staff and Micro-Tech employees inside.

"Well, you heard the boss. Have fun and a great lunch," Thomas said while giving me a meal ticket coupon. "I will give the T-90X to Christopher."

"Thanks," I said. It was like talking to a different person again, since this Thomas was the familiar cheerful one.

The Book of Dreams

I looked around the cafeteria and only saw pork and meat

options. There was nothing I could eat. I stood there

disappointed with the meal ticket in hand.

strong suit."

STORY 2 — ISLA DEL DIABLO

The plane approached the island under the clear, cloudless sky. Unmapped and unexpected, this was a new discovery. Inside the plane, a man sat by the window, staring out through his binoculars.

"And what is this island called again?" he asked.

"The locals call it Isla Del Diablo," his companion, Humphrey, replied.

"Diablo, Humphrey? What does that mean?"

The Book of Dreams

"Devil, sir."

The man chuckled. "Devil? Well, bloody hell, what a name!"

"Charles, are you sure about landing here?"

"Absolutely. Who knows what treasures could be waiting? Land the plane!"

Charles loved exploration. Since childhood in the late 1800s, he had been captivated by tales of famous explorers and treasure hunters. Now, finally having his adventure, he dreamed of headlines like: "Discovery of 1930: Charles Huntington Unearths Lost Island Brimming with Riches." His imagination brought a greedy smile to his face.

As they exited the plane into the sweltering humidity, the lush greenery of the island greeted them. Charles, donned in an explorer's outfit, matched his

The Book of Dreams

excitement with his outfit, while Humphrey, inadequately dressed, wore a white suit.

"Shall we bring the rifle, sir?" Humphrey asked.

"Better be safe than sorry. You never know what we might encounter here. Let the pilot know we'll be gone a few hours, we don't want him leaving without us."

"I've already informed him, sir."

"Good man, Humphrey. I don't know what I'd do without you."

"Thank you, sir. But I'll accompany you."

"Very well, let's be off then."

After an hour of trudging through the dense forest, the humidity took its toll. Charles was thrilled by their journey, while Humphrey, his dress shoes muddied, tolerated it for the potential historical discovery.

The Book of Dreams

"Having a map would be nice. At least we have the sun for direction," Charles observed, pointing at the sun. "We must be heading east."

"Sir, the sun is setting. We have about three hours before..."

"Never mind that, Humphrey. Let's just venture a little farther."

The ground suddenly trembled beneath them, as if the island itself protested their intrusion. Humphrey stepped back cautiously, while Charles steadied himself.

"Sir, we should return to the plane."

Charles, however, remained unfazed and curious. "Let's keep going."

But the ground gave way beneath him, and he fell into an abyss. Humphrey shouted his name, staring into the void where Charles had vanished.

"Charles! Are you all right?"

The Book of Dreams

The silence was his answer. Humphrey's anxiety grew. He wondered how he would explain this tragedy to Charles' family and friends.

"Charles! Can you hear me?"

"I'm here! Humphrey, you have to see this! It's amazing!"

Humphrey's heart leaped with relief. Charles was alive and seemingly unhurt.

"Are you all right, sir?"

"I need a torch and a rope."

"I'll fetch them. Please wait."

An hour later, Humphrey returned with the equipment. He worried about the rope's length. As the sun began to set, they had no time to spare.

"Sir, I have what you asked for."

"About time! We're running out of time."

Carefully, Humphrey descended into the pit. The torches illuminated a stunning cavern. Startled bats fluttered out

The Book of Dreams

of the hole, and the gems that adorned the walls sparkled like eyes watching them.

"My, this goes on for miles! Look at these gemstones!" Charles marveled, his torch revealing a corridor shimmering with crystals.

Their excitement was interrupted by a cold breeze. At the tunnel's end, they discovered a tomb covered in gemstones. It depicted a hybrid creature with goat-like legs, a round face, and two ruby eyes.

"Sir, it's getting chilly," Humphrey noted.

"Indeed. What's that down there?" Charles asked, shining his torch at a shape.

At the tunnel's end stood a large tomb adorned with gemstones. But what caught their attention were the gemstone-encrusted walls, forming a design of the same peculiar creature.

"Sir, this is extraordinary. Look!"

The Book of Dreams

Their excitement escalated as they explored the cavern.

The wind whispered through the tunnel, and the walls

began to shift.

"What's that?" Charles pointed his torch at a strange

shape.

At the end of the corridor lay a tomb. Gemstones covered

the casket, adorned with the same creature they had seen

before. Charles and Humphrey approached the casket with

mixed emotions—excitement and anxiety.

"Shall we open it?" Charles asked.

Humphrey hesitated, a sense of foreboding weighing on

him. "Sir, perhaps we should return with a proper team?

What if it contains something malevolent?"

"Nonsense, Humphrey! We're the first to discover this. We

must open it together."

After the casket's heavy lid scraped open, it revealed

nothing but emptiness. No riches, no mummified body—

The Book of Dreams

just space. But in the corner, a small ruby gemstone glinted.

"Sir, what's that?" Humphrey gasped.

Charles, intrigued, picked up the gemstone. It was smooth and oval-shaped.

"What could this be?" Charles wondered.

Humphrey studied the gemstone and found a Coptic inscription. After deciphering it, he grew uneasy.

"Sir, I think we should leave this behind. The inscription speaks of evil."

"Evil? Humphrey, this is a discovery of a lifetime! We can't leave it behind."

Humphrey's voice trembled. "Sir, please, we can't take it. It's cursed."

Charles, however, scoffed at his friend's apprehension. He decided to test the gemstone himself.

"I wish to have all the riches in the world," he proclaimed.

The Book of Dreams

Nothing happened. Charles smirked and brushed off Humphrey's concerns. But as they argued, the gemstone began to glow.

"Sir, stop! It's too dangerous!" Humphrey warned.

Ignoring Humphrey's protests, Charles refused to part with the gemstone. Their disagreement escalated into a struggle, and Charles found himself falling into the chasm with the gemstone in hand.

"Humphrey, help me!" Charles yelled as he disappeared into the darkness.

Humphrey shouted his friend's name, his voice echoing in the cavern. But it was futile.

"Charles, can you hear me?" Silence.

Humphrey mourned the loss of his friend, convinced that the gemstone had claimed him. He exited the cavern alone, the gemstone left behind.

2030—100 years later

The Book of Dreams

"What's the name of this island again?" Jim asked.

"Isla del Diablo," Katherine replied.

They explored a cave, their flashlights revealing a long

catacomb.

"This place gives me the creeps," Jim admitted.

"Look, what's this?" Jim reached into a tomb and pulled

out a red gemstone.

The Book of Dreams

STORY 3— NEIGHBORS

The assembly of homeowners gathered in the conference room, attired in 1950s suits and dresses. Their concern centered on a new neighbor moving into their neighborhood. Although their knowledge about this newcomer was limited, the one certainty was that they were unlike the residents.

"I'm sorry, Fred, but I can't accept this. I don't want them joining our neighborhood," asserted a man, seated in a wooden chair, puffing on a cigarette. His beady eyes glared from behind thick black-rimmed glasses.

"Tom, resisting change won't help. Their application was approved by the bank," responded Fred.

Sitting beside her husband, Frank, Mary sighed. "I can't believe this is happening. Right here, in our neighborhood, in this era."

"Mary's right," chimed in Sue, a kind and gentle elderly woman seated beside her. Her husband had passed away shortly after the war.

A chorus of voices joined the debate, neighbors expressing their opinions. A real estate agent stood before them, representing the client who had chosen not to attend.

"Everyone, please, let's calm down. Arguing won't solve anything. In fact, the decision has already been made. They're moving in, that's that," interjected Paul Baker, the banker. Once respected, his approval of the loan to these

The Book of Dreams

new neighbors had tarnished his reputation among the attendees.

"In this day and age! Yes, they're different from us, but consider what this might do to our property values!" Sue exclaimed. "I've lived in this town for over thirty years and never imagined this would happen, not in our town or our neighborhood."

Fred rose, directing his anger at Paul. "Sue's right! Property values will plummet if we allow them to settle here!"

Paul shook his head in exasperation. "You're misunderstanding. Look at this." He held up a newspaper article from a reputable publisher and writer. "Take a look at this," he urged, passing the paper around.

Once everyone had perused the article, Paul continued. "See? Values have actually risen! Having neighbors like this has enhanced the value."

The Book of Dreams

Whispers and conversations buzzed in the room, some residents swaying while others, like Franklin, remained skeptical.

"I don't know," Franklin ventured, adjusting his black fedora. At forty, he was the neighborhood heartthrob. "I've heard their skin is different from ours."

"What's that supposed to mean, Franklin?" Paul inquired, puzzled.

Franklin smirked. "I dated one."

Gasps and astonished murmurs rippled through the room.

"You did?" a woman seated at the back questioned.

"I did," Franklin admitted. "She was attractive. But whenever we were out, people stared. It was uncomfortable. We went on a few dates, but eventually, I had to end it. My parents weren't supportive either."

"I can't believe what I'm hearing," Mary scoffed.

The Book of Dreams

"And I was just about to tell my sister about you!" Franklin retorted, embarrassed by his own revelation. He swiftly left the room.

Paul implored, "Hold on, Franklin. There's no reason to be embarrassed."

Franklin glanced back, scoffing. "Easy for you to say."

"Now, let's all calm down," Paul urged, attempting to pacify the room. "Set aside your personal sentiments and think about it. They're like us in nearly every way."

Heads shook skeptically in response.

"I understand they might behave differently, but their intentions are peaceful. Have you heard stories about them committing crimes? Tell me, have you?"

A silence fell over the crowd as Paul's question resonated. They realized he had a point.

"No," Tom answered.

The Book of Dreams

"Her skin might've been different, but she was a lovely girl," Franklin added.

"Exactly! So give them a chance. They could teach you about humanity, even if they're not human."

"Fine, I'll give them a chance," Tom conceded.

Paul smiled. "And what about the rest of you?"

Franklin resumed his seat. "I'll give them a chance, and I'll give Maggie a call."

"Wait, is her name Maggie Q?" Mary inquired.

"Yes."

"I've heard about her! She's a bit quirky, but I never knew you dated her."

"Come on, it was just a few dates," Franklin explained.

"But Paul's right. Life's too short to hold onto such prejudice. Even if they are... well..."

"Go on, say it," Fred encouraged. "Say what they are. Robots. Damn robots! I don't care what anyone says. I was

The Book of Dreams

born just after the third war, and I don't want a fourth

with these... things." Fred stormed out, with other

homeowners following suit. Some remained unconvinced,

others were tentative, more open to the idea of robot

neighbors. Paul shook his head and gathered his

belongings.

"Excuse me, sir?" a young boy approached Paul.

"I think what you did today was great. Thank you! Too

many older folks struggle with change."

Paul smiled at the young blond-haired boy. "Thank you,

Timmy. But we shouldn't reveal our secret. The town

would be in turmoil if they discovered we're robots."

"Don't worry, Paul, I won't tell anyone who we truly are."

"Thank you, Timmy. I hope people like you will learn to see

AI creations with open hearts and minds."

"Maybe one day humans will embrace change with open

minds. Maybe one day they'll see with their hearts rather

The Book of Dreams

than their eyes. They're quick to resort to violence but

rarely choose love," Timmy added.

Paul smiled as Timmy dashed away, hoping for a future

where robots and humans could coexist harmoniously.

STORY 4 - SHATTERED CLOUDS

"I don't know why I'm flying with this airline again," the woman rudely muttered. She stood in the aisle, waiting for the passengers in front of her to take their seats. "Yes, this is probably the worst airline," she added.

The passenger in front of her shook his head, continuing to stow his belongings in the overhead compartment. He sighed in frustration and settled into the middle seat between two other passengers. One of them, a man who appeared to be in his twenties, smiled politely, while the other, a young woman, remained engrossed in her cell phone.

As the remaining passengers settled in and fastened their seat belts, a loud ding resonated through the cabin. The plane was preparing to taxi on the runway. While safety instructions blared over the intercom, most passengers paid them no heed, their attention glued to their phones. Inside the cockpit, the captain conducted final checks while the co-pilot guided the plane onto the runway. It was mid-July, and most passengers were on a holiday journey. Today's flight was bound for London from Miami. The Miami airport buzzed with activity, typical of a Friday morning.

Moments later, the plane began its ascent down the runway, ready to embark on its journey into the sky. Fluffy white clouds appeared, harmless and serene. The engines

The Book of Dreams

roared and whined as the aircraft sped down the runway, soaring into the sky. Passengers settled in as the plane climbed to its cruising altitude.

"Okay, folks, we've reached our cruising altitude. You can turn on your laptops and make yourselves comfortable," the captain's voice filled the cabin. He engaged the autopilot and relaxed in his seat.

A distinguished-looking man in a sport coat glanced at his seatmate, a man in his forties sporting a hoodie. He scoffed at the sight, considering it strange for someone his age to wear a hoodie. Sensing the stare, the hoodie-wearing passenger turned to him, prompting the man to smile awkwardly. The response was met with a cold glare.

"Need something?" the hoodie-wearer asked.

The man cleared his throat. "No, just admiring your hoodie."

The Book of Dreams

"Really? From the look on your face, it seemed like you were thinking something else. You got a problem with how I look?"

Caught off guard, the man struggled to respond. An airline employee passed by and sensed the tension between them.

"Is everything okay here?" she inquired.

"Yeah, Carol, we're fine," the distinguished man replied, noting her name tag.

"Alright. If you need anything, just..."

A sudden bout of turbulence jolted the plane, flinging the employee onto the hoodie-wearer's lap. He caught her in a surprisingly intimate pose, their eyes meeting as they exchanged a smile. The distinguished man's expression shifted, a mix of disgust and perhaps jealousy.

"Sorry about that," Carol apologized, blushing.

The Book of Dreams

"It's no problem. I'm Zach. What about you?" the hoodie-wearer said.

"Carol. As my name tag suggests."

"Right, sorry," Zach stammered.

"Thanks for saving me," she said.

Another round of turbulence followed, milder this time.

Carol managed to steady herself using a seat's headrest.

"I feel like a drunken sailor," she admitted. "I'd better sit down."

The captain's announcement interrupted the scene. "I apologize, folks. We've hit some rough patches. Not sure what's going on. Wait a moment..."

In the cockpit, the two pilots scrutinized their radar. A peculiar cloud was approaching – unlike any storm. It was a harbinger of something far worse.

"What's that?" a passenger exclaimed, staring out the window.

The Book of Dreams

A grayish-white cloud enveloped the plane, triggering intense turbulence. Panic erupted among passengers as they cried out, screamed, prayed. The seatbelt sign blazed, the sunlit sky darkening as the plane plunged. Chaos reigned as the emergency oxygen masks dropped, the passengers gripping armrests, bracing for the end.

The rude woman, regretting her choice of airline, defied the seatbelt warning, catapulting forward and striking the distinguished man, killing him instantly. Amid the turmoil, debris splattered onto a window as someone succumbed to sickness. A horrifying scene unfolded.

The plane leveled off, oxygen masks still worn, survivors reeling. Zach, now wearing his mask, gazed at Carol. She moved toward him, settling into the seat beside him. He removed his mask and sighed.

"Are you okay?" Carol inquired.

The Book of Dreams

Zach's eyes met hers, and he smiled weakly. "Yeah, I am.

Just never seen anything like this."

The announcement from the captain shattered the silence.

"Attention, everyone. I apologize for the trauma. The

cloud you saw was from a nuclear explosion over

Washington D.C."

Chaos and sobbing intensified. Carol's friend in San

Francisco weighed heavily on her. Zach tried to comfort

her. "We're alive; that's what matters."

The captain's voice cut through again. "We'll attempt an

emergency landing. Airforce escort is coming. Stay calm."

The hum of turbines accompanied their aimless flight.

Inside the bathroom, Zach glimpsed something unnerving

in the mirror, fleeing in alarm. Back in the cabin,

passengers and crew succumbed to oxygen deprivation,

death's grip tight.

The Book of Dreams

"Sir," a pilot's voice sounded from a nearby jet. "Everyone is dead. Autopilot kept us flying. They ran out of oxygen."

Zach's mind raced, finding solace only with Carol. They moved to the back, the sight of deceased passengers unsettling. The escort's arrival seemed distant.

"Everyone's dead," Carol whispered.

Zach held her, speechless, eyes cast out to a surreal, ominous sky. As the escort approached, survivors' thoughts turned to home, a world reeling from chaos.

"Attention," the captain's voice reassured. "Escort's here. Stay seated."

The plane hummed, its course uncertain, Zach's thoughts focused on Carol. As their conversation meandered, Zach pondered life's fragility. With a nod to each other, they steeled themselves for what lay ahead, together in a world transformed by catastrophe.

The Book of Dreams

STORY 5 — THE FACELESS DOLL FROM

CONSTANTINOPLE

People used to fight for honor and glory, driven by

ideals that transcended material gains. However, in the

present era, battles are waged for the allure of money and

possessions. The clash of swords and the flight of arrows

have surrendered to the thunderous sounds of guns and

rockets. Lives, once extinguished through physical

engagement, now meet their end with a mere press of a

The Book of Dreams

button. In today's warfare, the emergence of heroes whose names will echo through history is a rarity.

Amid the obsidian expanse of night, a lifeless body was deposited onto the shoreline. This figure, garbed in a wetsuit marked by bullet holes and stained with blood, seemed almost an inconspicuous relic of some past calamity.

But the veiled hours of darkness did not cloak him entirely; a woman's gaze found him, a serendipitous savior in the dimness. She discovered his unconscious form, clinging tenaciously to life's fleeting thread. The woman's determination led her to drag his battered frame to her waiting red Subaru, its presence a lone sentinel on the beach's edge. Within him, fragmented memories danced - the ebb and flow of the waves, an aquatic odyssey guided by a fate defined by danger. A trail of blood betrayed his journey from the clutches of a failed mission.

The Book of Dreams

Within the confines of the woman's apartment, the sanctum of salvation took shape. With skillful hands, she attended to his wounds, stitching the gaping reminders of confrontation. The man, shrouded in unconsciousness, remained oblivious to the remedial efforts performed upon him. Scenes of the tumultuous sea voyage played before his mind's eye - the haunting crescendo of gunfire, the spectral dance of azure flashes.

Finally, amidst this sensory barrage, consciousness found its foothold. The man's eyes fluttered open, and a figure, framed by the hues of early dawn, stood before him. The woman's emerald eyes bore into his obsidian orbs, a moment of connection pulsating between them. "Where... am I?" he inquired, his voice a faint whisper. "In my apartment," she replied, her voice carrying a soothing cadence.

The Book of Dreams

Beyond the room's confines, the call of the morning prayer permeated the air, a gentle reminder of the city awakening to its daily rhythm. Light breached the horizon, painting the world in shades of gold. Logan's stomach growled, an unexpected intrusion on his attempt to grasp his surroundings.

"What city is this? I hear..."

"This is Istanbul. The morning prayer," she explained, her voice carrying the resonance of a practiced familiarity.

"Istanbul?" he echoed, grappling with the notion. "How did I get here? Where was I found?"

"You washed ashore. Wounded. I removed the bullets," she stated matter-of-factly.

"Wounded? I was shot?" His fingers grazed the bandages that concealed the wounds.

"Yes. Miraculously, you survived. What's your name?"

The Book of Dreams

"I can't recall," he admitted, a touch of frustration coloring his response. "And you?"

"Kira. And you?"

He shook his head, his memory still a nebulous void. "I don't remember."

Gently, she offered a small bag containing a fragment of his identity, an assortment of passports from diverse nations, currencies that spanned continents, and a handgun. Yet, it was the nondescript flash drive that seized his attention, a harbinger of enigmatic truths.

"What did you uncover?" she inquired.

Choosing discretion, he closed the file he'd opened on the laptop and surreptitiously pocketed the flash drive.

Looking up at her, he revealed a smile and replied, "Not much, really."

The Book of Dreams

Kira's intrigue was palpable, her curiosity pressing for

more. Logan's guarded nature found its mark as he shook

his head and relinquished the laptop.

"That's about all," he responded.

Breakfast passed in silence, the minimalistic space

of the apartment dictating their proximity. A small wooden

table cradled their shared meal, a space for sustenance

and conversation. As they finished, Logan felt the weight

of his mission pressing upon him - his need to ascertain

Kira's true identity.

"May I ask a favor?" he ventured.

"Of course, anything," Kira replied with genuine openness.

"Do you have a tattoo?" he posed, his eyes discreetly

assessing the butter knife within reach.

The moment she turned her back to him, he acted. The

butter knife, an improvised weapon, lay ready for his

grasp. Simultaneously, her response resounded, her

The Book of Dreams

admission of a tattoo painting a vivid image of a crescent-shaped scar. The scar, the mark of his target, transformed her from a savior to the hunted.

"Well? What's your take?" she queried, unaware of his inner turmoil.

"It's intriguing," he responded, fighting to suppress his turmoil.

Kira moved with a grace that belied her true nature. She lunged, and Logan's reflexes responded, the butter knife serving as an unlikely shield against her initial assault. But the bizarre events that followed, the speed of her movements and the alien green fluid that oozed from her wounds, shattered his understanding of reality.

His recollections resurfaced, an echo of a directive to eliminate the "faceless doll of Constantinople." Memories merged with reality as Kira's onslaught continued. Conflicting emotions surged, but Logan knew his duty.

The Book of Dreams

As Kira fell, her body bleeding the unnatural green substance, Logan's breaths came ragged and uneven. Her eyes, once human, bore the semblance of something otherworldly.

"What are you?" he demanded, his voice laden with incredulity and disbelief.

Kira's response never came. In her silence, Logan's confrontation with the enigma that was Kira concluded, leaving the crimson pool of her blood as the haunting evidence of his choices.

A week later, a meeting with his commanding officer marked the aftermath of his mission.

"You accomplished your mission, Logan."

"What was she, sir?" Logan's voice resonated with a mixture of bewilderment and curiosity.

"That's information classified for now. But rest assured, we must uncover more like her and thwart their ambitions."

The Book of Dreams

"Why?" Logan's query carried an underlying sense of

urgency.

"They seek to conquer our world, Logan."

The Book of Dreams

STORY 6 — BROKEN WATERS

"I'm heading to the new fish market today. Need anything from there?"

"Sure thing, Josh. Grab some shrimp, but make sure they're shelled. Easier to cook."

"Got it, Monica. Shrimp without shells. Anything else?"

"What are you planning to get?"

Josh smirked at his wife. "Maybe a tiger shark?"

Monica chuckled. "Doubt they're selling those there."

The Book of Dreams

"Well, you never know! I'll also pick up some salmon and maybe an octopus."

"Octopus? Can you even cook that?"

"I can, my friend from Greece taught me."

"Oh right, I forgot about him. What was his name again?"

"Kostas," he replied.

"Ah, right. I hope I meet him someday. You talk about him all the time, but I've never met him."

Josh brushed off his wife's comment, laughing as he left the apartment.

Despite it being late July, the air was crisp. The bustling streets were full of life, with people and vehicles moving about. A crow perched on a branch observed Josh as he walked, contemplating his seafood purchases and the market's freshness. The store had only opened two days ago, with scarce online reviews to rely on.

The Book of Dreams

Josh arrived at the newly opened fish market after a brisk walk. The entrance lacked a sign, suggesting it was still a work in progress. Inside, an older man stood behind a glass counter. He reminded Josh of his Greek friend's father.

"Welcome, come in!" the man greeted him warmly.

"Thank you. It's my first time here," Josh replied.

"Is that so? Well, how about a first-time discount? Twenty percent off on anything you like."

Josh smiled. "That's alright, you don't have to."

"No, I insist," the man interrupted. "And what's your name?"

"I'm Josh. And you?"

"Dimitri. My name's Dimitri. Feel free to look around, let me know if you need help."

"Thank you," Josh said.

The store impressed Josh with its decor and variety of seafood. Besides different fish, there were exotic choices

The Book of Dreams

like squid, conch, and an unusually large octopus. The

creature hung from a hook, seemingly lifeless until it

twitched slightly.

"What's that?" Josh pointed at the octopus.

"That?" Dimitri nodded at it. "It's an octopus. Ever tried

one? They're great on the grill."

Josh was taken aback. "I've seen and eaten octopus, but

not like that."

Dimitri chuckled, rubbing his salt-and-pepper beard.

"You're right. This might be an unusual one. Tell you what,

you can have it for thirty dollars."

The creature, large enough to feed a big family, intrigued

Josh. It did look different from a regular octopus. Upon

closer inspection, he noted its eight tentacles, a smooth

dark gray body, and a warm skin. He wondered if it was

still alive. Dimitri began sweeping the floor, so Josh shifted

The Book of Dreams

his focus to the rest of his shopping list. Later, he found himself drawn back to the octopus.

"Help me," a strange voice echoed.

Suddenly, a sharp pain surged through Josh's head, and his ears rang. It was the octopus, attacking the cab driver telekinetically. Blood dripped from the driver's nose as he struggled with the pain.

"Look, whoever you are, get out of my cab now! This never happened!" the driver ordered.

Josh left the cab with the creature. On the pier, the creature revealed its name as Nagurrath, but Josh could call it Carl. It thanked him for saving it and offered him a wish. Josh hesitated before wishing for a million dollars.

"Are you certain about this wish?" the creature asked.

"Yes, a million dollars could change my life," Josh replied.

"Your wish is granted. You will find it at home. I must return to my planet."

The Book of Dreams

As the creature dived into the ocean, a million

bucks appeared in the form of actual male deer, creating

chaos on the street. Hours later, as Josh returned in a cab,

the street was still covered with bucks.

"Something's up ahead. A bunch of deer or something,"

the driver complained.

Josh saw the bucks, realizing his wish had come true. He

chuckled, amazed by the unexpected turn of events.

The Book of Dreams

STORY 7 — THE SENTINEL

I checked into the hotel room after finally arriving, late due to an unexpected delay. It had been a long day filled with flight delays and missed connections. Though the storm had passed, my fatigue and weariness still lingered. The woman at the front desk checked me in without any issue or questions, which provided some relief. The room was quaint, despite being designed for a single occupant. Midnight was approaching as my head finally touched the soft, fluffy pillow. My mind continued

The Book of Dreams

to wander, stressed from the day's events. This was my first time staying at this hotel in New Orleans, and I was eager to start my exploration of the infamous French Quarter the next day.

As I drifted off to sleep, a strange noise of fumbling and the turning of the doorknob startled me awake. I opened my eyes and saw a woman dressed in a white nightgown standing before the door. Her image flowed beneath the yellow streetlight that streamed into the room. Her appearance was almost ghostly as she stared silently at me, her eyes penetrating through her strands of light brown hair.

"Who are you and how did you get in here?" I asked, my voice uncertain.

The woman remained silent, her gaze unwavering.

I repeated my question as I sat up and continued staring at her.

The Book of Dreams

"Through the window," she finally replied, her voice soft but carrying a strange resonance.

I looked over at the window, and to my surprise, I found it closed and undisturbed. A feeling of confusion settled in. I walked over to the window and inspected it closely; the thin layer of dust on the sill and frame remained untouched. Either the woman was lying, or there was more to her presence than met the eye. When I turned around, she was gone.

An unsettling mix of feelings stirred within me, a ghastly fear accompanied by a cold chill. I stood still and silent beneath the ticking clock, grappling with the uncertainty. Logic fought for my attention, telling me that this was a product of my imagination, perhaps residual sleepiness. I returned to my bed, trying to shake off the unease and fall back asleep.

The Book of Dreams

Some unknown time later, I was awakened again by the same peculiar sound. I slowly opened my eyes and sat up, only to find the woman standing beside my bed, staring down at me. Startled, I nearly tumbled off the other side of the bed, clutching the sheets tightly as if they were a protective shield.

"What are you doing?" I asked, my voice a mixture of fear and confusion.

The woman's presence unsettled me as much as before.

"Sleep," I responded, my voice trembling.

"What?" she questioned.

"Sleeping," I clarified, clearing my throat. "I was sleeping, but you startled me. How did you get into my room?"

The woman continued to stand silently, her gaze locked onto me.

"I entered through the window," she replied, her tone just as enigmatic as before.

The Book of Dreams

"Through the window? But I checked the window, and it was untouched," I protested.

"Because I traveled through it," she answered matter-of-factly.

Her words sent a shiver down my spine. Was this woman truly an apparition? Yet, my logical side reassured me that this was just a dream, a product of my overactive mind.

"How?" I finally managed to ask.

"I can travel through many things. So can you," she said.

My skepticism compelled a scoff. "That's preposterous."

"Come with me," she gestured, her voice carrying an air of urgency.

"Wait," I interjected. "Let me change out of my nightwear."

Standing before the hotel room door, locked and closed, I stared at the woman beside me. I felt certain she

The Book of Dreams

couldn't see her. I held her hand, and as we walked through the door, I closed my eyes, waiting for the transition to end.

"Follow me," she directed.

Together, we climbed the stairwell in darkness, each step quiet and soundless. My grip on her hand was the only thing guiding me. We reached a destination, and when I opened my eyes, I found myself standing in front of a small apartment building.

"Did you grow up here?" I inquired, still uncertain about the situation.

"I did," she confirmed. "I loved it here."

Numerous questions begged for answers, but reluctance held me back. I wondered how this woman had died.

"I was murdered," she suddenly revealed.

Startled, I looked around, making sure no one had heard her words.

The Book of Dreams

"You were?"

"Yes," she said, her voice echoing with an unearthly quality.

Two women passed by, giving us curious looks, and I couldn't help but wonder if they'd heard her confession.

"You can hear my thoughts?" I asked.

She nodded subtly, a knowing expression on her face.

"We've arrived," she declared.

Standing in front of a small apartment building, she gestured toward the entrance. A sense of unease crept over me. I knew what she wanted, but entering a stranger's home at this hour seemed inappropriate and intrusive.

"Did you grow up here?" I asked Samantha. Her ghostly appearance seemed even more out of place in the vibrant French Quarter.

The Book of Dreams

"I did," she answered, her voice carrying a nostalgic tone.

"I loved it here."

I struggled with the ethical implications of entering the building. It was a decision that went against my usual nature, yet the sense of urgency in Samantha's demeanor pulled me in.

"May I ask a favor?" she said softly.

My skepticism grew, but her vulnerability convinced me to listen.

"Sure," I responded cautiously.

"Please stand up."

I stood up as Samantha directed. An unsettling sensation washed over me as I felt her presence inch closer. Her spirit seemed to envelop me, intertwining with my consciousness. Images and memories flowed through my mind, Samantha's life flashing before my eyes. I saw her as a carefree child, playing with her parents and

The Book of Dreams

relishing her mother's Italian cooking. The scenes shifted,
revealing her struggles as a teenager and the arguments
that had driven her away from home.

Before I knew it, I was speaking with Samantha's
voice, recounting her life to her parents. I felt their
emotions—their disbelief, grief, and eventual
acceptance—as Samantha's memories became mine. Her
mother gasped, her father dropped to his knees, and my
heart swelled with a mixture of compassion and sorrow.

Samantha's story poured out, revealing the tragic
events leading to her death. She had been murdered, her
life cut short in a cemetery. I found myself offering
comfort and closure to her parents, relaying Samantha's
final messages and conveying her love for them.

As her story concluded, the weight of her emotions
lifted from me. I stood before Samantha's parents, feeling

The Book of Dreams

both a sense of accomplishment and a deep connection to the young woman.

"You brought her to us!" Samantha's father exclaimed, his voice filled with gratitude.

Tears streamed down her mother's cheeks as she embraced me. "Thank you!"

"Jonathan," Samantha's voice called out to me. "Thank you. I am at peace now. You have a gift, a connection to the other side. You are the sentinel of the dead."

With Samantha's gratitude echoing in my mind, I left her parents' home, feeling a profound sense of purpose. My encounter with the supernatural had left me changed, connected to a world beyond our own.

The Book of Dreams

STORY 8 — MIDORI

The men in suits always made decisions for us.

Their decisions were never in our best interest, even

though they claimed otherwise. This proved true after

they pioneered the creation of a new "super green," as

they called it. Also known as a scientific and medical

breakthrough, this new edible green vegetable was simply

called "midori," the Japanese word for green. Midori was a

scientific achievement that the world powers proudly

stood behind. Little did they know that their miracle was
The Book of Dreams

about to backfire, causing life-altering events that would

forever change our society and world.

Fortunately, not everyone was eager to jump on

the midori bandwagon. Those who did were the first to

experience the unexpected change. It went unnoticed at

first, until the change started spreading like wildfire. Those

who ate the midori became known as "no-blinkers" since

they never blinked their eyes. This made it easy to

distinguish between humans and those affected. I write

this as a warning to stay awake and avoid consuming

midori.

Six Months Earlier

The television blared at deafening levels in the

small living room of the bungalow. An elderly woman sat

with her eyes fixed on the screen, showing a newscaster

The Book of Dreams

dressed in a red dress. Her slim figure stood next to a man in a cliché white lab coat. He held the newly created vegetable, midori, up to the camera for everyone to see. The newscaster, Julia, was equally impressed and smiled brightly.

"That looks delicious! Can I have a bite?" Julia kindly asked on air.

The scientist chuckled and nodded. "Of course! This is the healthiest vegetable. It is completely edible and safe. There are no side effects," he declared, facing the camera.

No side effects. That statement turned out to be wrong shortly after. Julia was the first to be infected. It did not take much convincing after the newscast to see the country adopt the newly green leafed vegetable. Salads in restaurants and fast-food joints across America were filled with it. Commercials sprung up promoting the health benefits and low-cost value. Soon, salads lost their "extras," containing only midori. People were ditching red meats and labeling themselves midori vegans. A new group emerged, turning into the true enemy.

Those who didn't eat the green leafy vegetable were deemed enemies. Riots broke out along with civil unrest. Their eyes remained open and fixated on consuming more midori while converting the deemed "unhealthy." It was a sadistic nightmare. There were moments when I almost gave in to temptation. Friends were filling their bowls with it and trying to share their portions with me. It had a strange aroma, reminiscent of sweet succulent honey.

Someone told me that the scent of midori depended on a person's favorite food. Their taste buds only experienced what they loved. Odd as it sounded, it made sense why there was such a craze for this vegetable. I wasn't the only one turned off by the strange

The Book of Dreams

phenomenon. My girlfriend, Veronica, wasn't interested in trying it either.

Despite her family succumbing to it and filling their recipe books, my girlfriend and I abstained. At family parties, every dish except ours contained midori. Even desserts were made with it, no surprise given the growing fanaticism. It took a month for my entire city to become nearly obsessed. This is where our trouble began.

"Lock the door," I told Veronica after entering our apartment. I pushed the shopping cart inside. The wheels squeaked as if struggling under the weight of numerous water bottles. I used one hand as a support to keep the cases from toppling over like a shaky building during an earthquake.

"Did you buy enough?" she sarcastically asked, locking the door.

I gave her an impatient look and shook my head.

The Book of Dreams

"Fortunately, essentials were aplenty, thanks to everyone focusing on the midori."

"How is it out there?" Veronica questioned while helping me dismantle the water bottle tower.

"It's still relatively tame. I wore my mask so no one could tell if I was a Midorian or not. That's what they call themselves now."

"This is getting out of hand. What are we going to do?"

I looked at Veronica, seeing worry on her face.

"I'm sure this will blow over eventually," I answered, uncertain. I could tell she sensed my uncertainty too, as she looked at me skeptically.

"Okay, you're right. But luckily, we have enough to last us for months now. Plus, we're growing our own herbs and vegetables. We still have running water." I turned on the faucet to confirm. "See?"

The Book of Dreams

"Even so, do you expect us to stay in here?" She looked around our small apartment.

"I know it's not ideal, but we have what we need. And, we know that even with the midori, those infected need water. Like all living things, they can't survive without it."

"Still. What if they try to get in here?"

Veronica's question left me flummoxed.

"I don't understand. Why would they try to get into our apartment? We have nothing of value."

"You don't get it, do you? They're trying to convert everyone. They're even beginning to destroy other essential foods and replace them with midori. If they find out we're not like them, I'm... I'm afraid, Keith."

"Come on, let's watch something on TV. I brought you some of those cookies you like, see?" I held up a box of vegan cookies.

The Book of Dreams

Veronica smiled. "Thanks. You're sweet for thinking of me."

I laughed. "Of course. I even got you tampons. In fact, I think you have a lifetime supply now!"

She laughed and threw a cookie at me as the news anchor appeared on the screen.

"We're here outside Sir Shop-A-Lot, and as you can see, Larry, everyone's running in and tossing out all other non-essential food into the parking lot."

We watched the TV together as a mob rushed into the supermarket. The automatic doors struggled to stay open amidst the constant movement. People streamed in and out like addicts. They tossed out canned goods, other produce, and even bottled water. Disgusting and disturbing, they destroyed food in the name of their midori addiction. They were no longer themselves or human.

The Book of Dreams

"What a scene!" the reporter exclaimed. "Everyone's having a festive time, Larry. Excuse me, sir," the reporter stopped a man rushing into the store. "Are you here to participate in the purge?" The man looked nervous, smiling. "Yeah, I am," he answered. "Excuse me for a moment, Larry. We have a nonbeliever on our hands!" The woman grabbed the man, yelling "nonbeliever." Some in the mob turned and charged at him. They chanted "Midori" as they dragged him away, ignoring his pleas. The woman returned to the camera, smiling.

"Sorry about that, folks. You know how it is with nonbelievers. Larry, everyone has to have some midori," she added with a chuckle.

Larry, the middle-aged anchor, appeared on screen, grinning. "Sure do, Nicki. Sure do!"

The Book of Dreams

The woman was back on screen, accompanied by the man

who had been apprehended earlier. His wide eyes spoke

volumes.

"How do you feel now?" Nicki asked.

She grinned at him, and he spoke about being saved and

wanting to help others. Sickening to watch, it was clear we

were in danger. Our home wouldn't be safe for much

longer. We eventually had to leave for more provisions.

Six Months Later

It took six months to go through our provisions.

With winter upon us, we had to limit ourselves to smaller

meals, eating only once a day. The challenge grew given

the circumstances. Close calls had become routine, and

much of the city had transformed. More of them were out

there, constantly seeking people like us. I waited in my

The Book of Dreams

apartment for Veronica's return, several hours having passed since she ventured out for food. She insisted, despite my protests. I hoped her stubbornness wouldn't lead to her downfall.

I looked out the window, spotting a crowd approaching down the street. My heart sank, fear gripping me. I strained my eyes, hoping to catch a glimpse of Veronica, but she wasn't visible. I held on to a sliver of hope, a false sense of security. Like a child clings to a blanket in a relentless storm. But this storm was a rabid crowd, or something worse. These were no longer people; they were something else.

A heavy knock startled me, breaking my focus from the approaching crowd. My mind raced, wondering if it was Veronica, but she never knocked. Maybe it was one of them. I wanted to ignore it, but the noise might attract others. I cautiously approached the door, karambits in

The Book of Dreams

hand. I looked through the peephole and recognized my neighbor's son, Rodrigo, no older than twenty. He looked shaken, as if he'd seen a ghost. His blinking eyes indicated he was still human. I opened the door, seeing he wasn't alone. He stood there, breathless, with four friends dressed in winter attire.

"What's wrong, Rodrigo?"

"Keith," he gasped, struggling to breathe. "I saw her, captured at the grocery store down the street. Angry crowd's coming. We need to get out."

"What?" I stood like a statue, fear and regret overwhelming me. It should've been me. "Where is she? I'll rescue her."

"No. It's too late. They're coming for you. For us. She told them everything to save you."

A fury of hatred surged within me. I grabbed my go-bag and black jacket and followed them out of the building.

The Book of Dreams

Our boots echoed as we moved, like a determined platoon entering battle. But this wasn't a battle; it was survival. My thumbs rested in the ring handles of my curved blades. I was ready.

"I'm going to rescue her," I declared.

"Fine. But let's take the sewers. It's the only way," Rodrigo suggested.

We exited through the back entrance as the sounds of yelling and chanting grew from the other side. They were breaking into the building, our sanctuary, our former home. We ran down the street away from the building, toward the grocery store where Veronica was held. The sun was setting, and darkness was our ally. But the sound of the strange creature below could expose us.

"Go, get down there," Eric, one of Rodrigo's friends, ordered. He held the sewer cover over the opening.

The Book of Dreams

One by one, we climbed down the ladder into a puddle of wastewater. The stench was nauseating, but I was too focused on saving Veronica to care. The six of us advanced with our flashlights. Rats scattered as our beams hit them, as if they were magic wands. Water dripped, creating an unsettling echo. I wanted out of there.

"Did you hear that?" Eric asked from behind us. "A noise like someone's coming."

"I didn't hear anything. You're hearing things, Eric."

"Shut up, Carlos. You're deafer than a doorknob."

"Enough arguing. Go check it out if you're so concerned," I barked.

The two teenagers exchanged glances and moved into the shadows. Their flashlights faded, leaving us four behind. We pressed forward, getting closer to our destination. Suddenly, we heard yelling and screaming

The Book of Dreams

behind us. It was Carlos. He approached in a panic from behind.

"Go, get out of here! They're coming! Ahh!"

Reluctantly, I acted after protests from the others. I closed the sewer lid, leaving Carlos and Juan behind with the creature. The three of us - Rodrigo, Laura, and I - moved toward the grocery store. There were no lights inside, a sign of an ambush.

"This doesn't look good," Rodrigo said. "I'll stay out here and keep watch. Laura, go with Keith."

"Or, you could come with us!"

"Shut up and go. I have a gun; he only has knives."

I wanted to join the argument but stayed silent. Laura and I entered the small grocery store together. Thin shelves were packed with nothing but midori. They must've held other items before, but all we could see with our flashlights were the leafy greens.

The Book of Dreams

"This stuff's everywhere," Laura whispered.

Ignoring her comment, I focused on finding Veronica. We reached the back of the store, where a woman sat bound and blindfolded. She muffled noises, but I couldn't understand. It was Veronica. After freeing her, we embraced. Reuniting was a relief. Rodrigo entered the store cautiously.

"Great, you found her. Now we can get started," he said.

"Started with what?" Laura asked, approaching him with her gun raised.

He laughed. "What are you going to do, shoot me? Even if you do, it won't change anything. You'll still..."

Before he could finish, Laura fired two shots from her revolver. Green fluid oozed from his wounds as he screamed an unearthly sound. His agony activated nearby midori leaves, which formed into a plant. The plant grew into an octopus-like creature with thorny vines. Laura yelled and fired more shots, but the creature's tentacles killed her.

"Veronica, get out!" I yelled.

"Why? What's the point?"

I turned and saw Veronica, my beloved, smiling wickedly.

Her eyes remained open as she laughed evilly.

STORY 9 — GODS IN THE SAND

Out here in the desert, things can easily be forgotten, swallowed into the endless waves of still sands. Lost wanderers can become forgotten memories covered away for countless years. The man, Argo Maximus, is one such lost wanderer who escaped from one prison only to end up in another. Distant sands fill an endless horizon beneath a piercing hot sun that hangs over him. Starving birds circle high above, waiting for his last breath.

The Book of Dreams

His life was not always like this. He had a family, but they were taken from him all too soon. He smiles to himself as he stares at the mirage. Palm trees that are not really there stand tall, awaiting his arrival. The two trees remind him of someone familiar, his two friends.

"Argo," said the man. "What are you waiting for? The crowd, they call your name. This is your moment."

Argo smiles at his friend. "Narib, you are always there by my side. This fight will be our last fight. We were never born for this life."

The man's words invoke light laughter from Narib. "Do you hear him, Malak? He is being a philosopher again."

Malak shakes his head. "We may not have been born to be gladiators, but sometimes life chooses a destiny we have always needed."

Argo shakes his head. "Why would we need to be gladiators? What good is this life?"

The Book of Dreams

Narib rubs the sweat off his smooth brow and bald head.

"We are heroes in their eyes. We are saviors."

"Saviors? What could we possibly be saving them from?"

Malak erupts in laughter. "Boredom."

Suddenly, the tall iron gates rise up. The loud churning of iron and chain informs them to ready themselves. Bright blinding sunlight pours in along with the dirt before them. As the three men make their way through the entrance to the massive coliseum, a loud eruption from the crowd fills the air around them. People from all over Rome and even as far as Constantinople have come; rumor has it, even as far as Babylon.

"Maximus! Maximus! Maximus!" the crowd chants as if Argo were some sort of god.

"Do you hear that? They're calling for you," said Narib. "Go now, you are their champion.

"You are a god among men," Malak adds.

The Book of Dreams

A light breeze touches Argo. His memory fades, and now he returns to the desert. The endless waves of sand fill his eyes with discouragement. He wonders when he will find his salvation. Specks of sand touch his short black hair. His white thin tunic is saturated in both sweat and memories from his past.

"Go, Argo, we will be right behind you," said Narib. Together, the men raise their weapons as the crowd grows louder. Malak holds his spear high up in the air while Narib bangs his axe against his wooden shield. Like a loud drum, the noise reverberates against the voices from the crowd. And as Argo lifts his arm up, the crowd stands together and cheers his name even louder.

The emperor, dressed in black, watches on with slight jealousy. He wants to see the men fall today, for it is only he who should be seen in this regard. It pains the emperor that the crowd idolizes this gladiator more than

The Book of Dreams

him. He growls beneath his breath and slowly stands up.

Gradually, the cheering fades, and their focus changes to

the emperor, who smiles and nods.

"If the three men before you win today," the emperor

pauses. "Then they will be free!"

His words cause another eruption, but this one is

much louder than before. The crowd loves this to their

heart's content. The emperor knows this is the only way

he would be rid of his champion. Through ninety-nine

fights, the three men have defeated some of his greatest

champions and warriors that walked this earth. From

feared Arcadians, Babylonians, Vikings, Germanians, and

even Spartans, the men have never lost a fight. The

previous fight was against Macedonia's most celebrated

warrior, Anton, who was rumored to have defeated ten

men with his bare hands. But Anton doesn't stand a

The Book of Dreams

chance against the three most celebrated gladiators to have ever graced his coliseum.

But today, the men will face their greatest and final warrior of all time. The feared warrior called the Scorpion. There's a rumor that he traveled from Persepolis. Scorpion carries no weapons other than his hands. He stands several feet taller than the three men, which gives him an advantage. His strength is unmatched, which will also work in his favor in this fight.

"Today, the men face their greatest challenge yet! I present to you their challenger, the Scorpion!"

As the Scorpion enters the coliseum, the crowd remains silent. They gasp at the sight of the gladiator as he steps beneath the sunlight. Beads of sweat roll down from his short hair. His muscular tan skin glistens as does his ceremonial blue and red armor, which looked to be made from the finest materials Persepolis has to offer.

The Book of Dreams

The three gladiators look at one another in a mixture of admiration and fear. They wonder where the emperor found such a man. But nonetheless, they know if they allow the man's intimidating stature, this would lead to their downfall. As Scorpion raises his fists into the air, the crowd remains silent until a few spectators cheer for his new opponent standing before them.

Argo sighs. His mouth, like the desert itself, is parched and yearning for the sweet nectar of water. With every step he takes, the sands cover his feet and sandals. The weight continues to take its toll on him. His body slowly grows weary. The mirage of the twin palm trees fades only to be replaced by another unexpected sight. A man covered in white rode toward him on a black steed. His face is wrapped in a white scarf, with only his eyes exposed. Argo wonders if this, too, is just another mirage.

The Book of Dreams

The memory from his last fight returns, and Argo continues reminiscing as he treks through the desert. His hands grip the handle of his short sword while his friends stand close beside him. Together, the three of them prepare themselves for what would be the fight of their lives. This moment would define them not only as warriors but as men because this opponent stands before their freedom.

"Are you ready, Argo?" Narib asks beneath the sea of cheers and chanting. The crowd continues calling out for Maximus, and now the Scorpion, who somehow gained some of his own followers.

"As ready as I will ever be. Malak, you attack from the right." Malak nods. Argo looks at Narib. "Flank from the left," he orders.

Together, the three men cautiously approach the man, who opens up his hands ready for their attack. He

The Book of Dreams

flashes a smile, which rests like a scorpion within a thick patch of shrubbery. The Scorpion's facial hair signifies a cliché of a battle-hardened warrior. Like a ravenous beast, the Scorpion is ready for Malak's charge. With ease, the warrior spins around the gladiator's spear and quickly drives his fist into the man's back. The impact from the unexpected hit leaves Malak wincing in heavy pain. It's strange because suddenly he loses feeling in his legs, forcing him onto the ground. Small rocks and dirt cover his knees and hands as the spear rests at his side.

Narib attempts to seize the opportunity by attacking the Persepolitan with his axe, which once belonged to a Viking that he killed in a previous match. However, the man is ready for his attack. It's almost as if the Scorpion could sense what the man is thinking. As Narib waves the weapon in a downward motion, the warrior counters with a front kick. The hard, wooden

The Book of Dreams

sandal presses against the gladiator's chest. The force from the impact sends the man onto the dirt with his axe falling beside him.

Surprised by the ease the Scorpion shows with countering the two gladiators' advances, Argo stands as the lone warrior before him. He smiles at Argo, who points his sword at him. The Scorpion kneels and lifts Malak's spear, which he stole from a Spartan after a previous fight.

The spectators cheer both warriors on as they face each other like two Goliaths. Blood escapes from Malak's mouth as he feels his heart slowly fading. Whatever the man did to him left him dying in pain. This is not how he expected his life to end, but he chuckles softly. He lived a long life beneath both the sun, the gaze of the emperor, and the admiration from his fans, who called him Malak the Merciful.

The Book of Dreams

Silently, the two men step sideways as their eyes remain focused on one another. Knowing he held the upper hand, the Persepolitan waves his hand at Argo. Despite the taunt, the gladiator remains headstrong and steady. He approaches the Scorpion on his own terms, tactfully and carefully. Beneath the noise of the crowd, Argo pounces forward like a lethal panther. The sword pierces an empty space because the Scorpion gracefully dodges the attack. He counters and strikes Argo's hand with his fist, forcing the weapon out from his grasp.

The blade falls almost as if it's in slow motion. Argo braces himself for his enemy's second attack. The Scorpion lunges and throws a hard-right hook at the man's face. Luckily, his helmet takes the majority of the blunt attack. But it leaves a large dent behind, forcing Argo to remove the damaged helmet.

The Book of Dreams

The Scorpion laughs arrogantly after realizing his opponent's helmet saved his life. Before Argo could counterattack, Narib charges and drives his shoulder into the man's chest. This unexpected attack leaves him slightly surprised. But despite his attack, the Scorpion stands tall right over him.

As Argo runs toward the men, the Scorpion plummets his elbow directly into the man's back. Even through his armor, Narib feels the piercing pain at the center of his spine. Within seconds, the Scorpion strikes again with his elbow, but this time aiming at the middle of the man's neck. Collapsing like a lifeless doll, Narib falls onto the dirt already dead at Argo's feet.

The man on the horse approaches closer to Argo, who realizes this is no mirage but an actuality. His horse huffs and whinnies as its hooves pierce the soft, scorching sand. At his side rests a scimitar while a long spear lays on

The Book of Dreams

his back. Recognizing Argo in the distance, the man grabs

his long spear and aims. Noticing the man gearing up for

an attack, Argo pauses in his tracks.

Sand billows around him as the golden rivers

temporarily separate the two men. With one swift throw,

the spear flies toward Argo like an angry falcon. With

whatever strength he could muster, the former gladiator

jumps forward onto the golden sand. He hears the spear

whiz over him, signaling it's safe to rise. As he does, the

horse stops before him, with the man staring down.

"I know who you are," the man says. Both his voice and

accent carry a familiarity. "You were once a famous

gladiator, were you not?"

Argo smiles. "Perhaps, but that was in another life."

"Another life?" the stranger questions. "If that is the case,

then what is this life?"

The Book of Dreams

"This life?" Argo asks. He holds out his tired arms and surveys the area. "This life is nothing more than a dying one."

"A dying one? But you look alive to me. You managed to dodge my spear. That is not something a dying man could ever do. I know who you are, Argo Maximus of Rome. Rumor has it you defeated countless men and heroes."

"All in the name of freedom."

Argo's remark brings laughter to the man. "More like glory. Your name lives on even in these forgotten sands. Come, let us finish our fight."

"Who are you?" Argo questions.

"Do you not remember me?"

Knowing their champion and hero was at the mercy of the Scorpion, the crowd begins chanting Maximus. The emperor smiles gleefully at the sight of events unfolding before him. Never did he expect to see Malak and Narib

The Book of Dreams

both defeated in a single fight. He salivates at the sight of

seeing Argo fall next; the thought excites him.

"I will not fall here, not today," declares Argo. "You may

have defeated my men, but you will not defeat me."

The Scorpion laughs. "Today will not be the day that you

fall. For today, you are already free. The emperor knows

what will happen if I kill you today."

"And what would happen?" Argo asks.

"They will riot and possibly kill me and him. I am not going

to defend that man for he is not my emperor!"

Both men look up at the emperor, who suddenly

realizes what they're discussing. Now faced with an

unexpected dilemma, the emperor knows he has to set

Argo free despite him not defeating the Scorpion. It leaves

him feeling disappointed, knowing he would not see the

death of the man today. But if Argo was to die today, then

The Book of Dreams

it would also mean his death. He's a celebrated champion and hero. The people love him like a god. Gods do not die.

"I know who you are," answers Argo. "We met many years ago. Our lives were both spared that day. You are a skilled warrior."

The Scorpion laughs as he jumps off his steed. "As are you. We never did finish our fight."

Argo exhales through his nostrils. "I suppose not. Do you want to finish it here? Now?"

The Scorpion looks around and notices the birds circling overhead. "No, the only witnesses are the hungry vultures. There is no glory in dying here today."

"Are you certain?"

The question leaves the Scorpion mystified. "I do not understand."

"If I kill you now, I will take your sword as my own. Your sword will be proof that I have killed you."

The Book of Dreams

"I suppose you have a point. If I win, then I will take your sword there," the warrior says, pointing his scimitar at Argo's weapon.

"So, what shall we do?" Argo questions.

"I suppose you are right, my friend. Let us do one final dance. But wait, what if we both die? Then?"

"Then our memory and legacy end here, today in these forgotten sands."

The Scorpion laughs. "Today a god will die!"

Both blades clash loudly within the sea of the desert, only to fall on deaf ears. There is no crowd or emperor to witness this spectacle but only a fight between two celebrated warriors. Two former gods who today would fall together as one.

The Book of Dreams

STORY 10 — THE APARTMENT

"I'm going to be gone for exactly one month," the man said over the phone.

"Okay. And you want me to stay here for the entire month?"

"Yeah, can you? I need someone to feed my cat, Mittons."

"Sure. Is it okay if my wife stays with me too? We both work remotely, so we could work from your apartment, if that's cool?"

The Book of Dreams

"Of course! I have really fast internet, so don't worry about that. I'll leave you plenty of food and some money in case you run out."

"Okay, thank you. You don't have to pay me for doing this, Travis."

"I know, David, but this is the least I can do. I'll give you four hundred when I return. The door code is 5398. There's something I should tell you about my apartment."

"What's that, Travis?"

"Yeah! Hold on! Sorry, man. I have to go. They're bugging me to get off the phone since we're about to take off. I'll be in Thailand, so I might not be able to respond, but reach out if you have any questions or problems. Talk to you later!"

And that was it. We had four weeks to spend in the apartment. It seemed simple enough and like a great mini getaway, even though Travis lived two hours away from

The Book of Dreams

me outside of Chicago. Tomorrow was the first week of February, so we had exactly twenty-eight days to stay there.

Week 1

"This is a nice place," my wife declared.

"I agree. It's a pretty spacious three-bedroom. I see Travis uses one room as an office, the other as his room, and the last one is the guestroom. This is where we'll be sleeping," I said, tossing my bag onto the black silk sheets.

"At least it's a king-size bed. Plenty of room to avoid your sharp elbows," my wife added.

I shook my head and scoffed. "Let's not compare sharp body parts," I said, pointing at my chin.

The Book of Dreams

She laughed and threw a pillow at me. "Is it me, or is it chilly in here?" she asked as we stepped out into the living room.

There was a large television hanging on the wall above the fireplace. The living room was nicely decorated with a glass coffee table, two leather couches, and a red Persian rug in the center. The walls were painted a royal blue. It felt like a comfortable bachelor pad.

"It is quite chilly in here, Amy," I answered. "Check to see if a window is open while I turn on the fireplace."

I knelt down and tinkered with the gas-powered fireplace. Outside, a gust of wind reminded me that it was still the dead of winter. Light snow fell, making living here this time of year feel like living in a snow globe.

"Ah, I found the culprit. The kitchen window was partly open. Weird. I wonder why he left it open?"

The Book of Dreams

"Probably to clear out the smell of farts. I don't know," I joked.

She rolled her eyes at me as she closed and locked the window. "Are you hungry? Let's eat."

"Good idea," my wife said while rummaging through the pantry. "Wow, he wasn't lying. He left us enough food to last us at least two months! I hope you like beans."

"Better open that window again then," I said.

The next morning, we woke up after spending our first night there. It was a standard first night. After dinner, we crashed on the couch and went to bed around midnight. It was quiet and comfortable sleeping there. I stepped out of bed and powered on my computer to start my day.

"Honey?"

"Yeah, babe, what's up?" I answered my wife.

The Book of Dreams

"Next time you open the window, can you please close it when you wake up? It's freezing in here again!"

I entered the kitchen and saw my wife closing the kitchen window again. It was a peculiar sight.

"Strange. I didn't open it last night. Did you?"

My wife looked at me and shook her head. "No. What? Are you sure? Maybe you did and don't remember?"

"Uh, no. We were together on the couch watching that terrible movie, remember? Then we crashed around midnight."

My wife remained silent. "Yeah. Well, maybe I did? I don't know. Regardless, let's keep this window closed."

"Good idea. Did you feed Mittons?" I asked her.

"Yeah. He likes this food." She sniffed the bag. "Ugh. This is disgusting. How do cats enjoy eating this trash?"

Mittons looked up at my wife and meowed softly, as if he agreed with her.

The Book of Dreams

The rest of the days flew by in a blur, as it was a busy week for both of us. Nothing strange happened in the apartment other than the kitchen window being open again on Thursday. I figured it was either my wife or me who opened it and couldn't remember. Amy worked about sixty hours because it was near tax season. She had a lot on her plate as a tax consultant. I am a web developer, so I had some deadlines that needed to be met. It was almost the end of the week, Sunday.

"Our first week has been quiet here," I declared to my wife. We sat on the couch together, watching a random movie.

"Yeah, other than work being busy, it was pretty good."

I held Amy close. "I'm glad we had a chance to get away."

She smiled at me, and we kissed.

Suddenly, something fell onto the kitchen floor, startling us both. It nearly made us jump off the couch in unison.

The Book of Dreams

My heart was beating and trembling simultaneously as we

looked at the kitchen area. The bluish glow from the

television screen illuminated the area, but it wasn't

enough to see clearly.

"What the hell was that?" Amy questioned.

"Probably the cat looking for food. Let me go and check it

out."

Amy stayed on the couch, watching me walk over

toward the kitchen, which was adjacent to the bathroom.

The wooden floor creaked beneath my footsteps. As I

approached the kitchen, I saw the light pouring from

beneath the slit of the bathroom door. A shadow slowly

passed as I stood in front of the door. After readying

myself, I clutched the cold doorknob and pushed it down.

I entered and saw the cat sitting on top of the toilet

seat. Its yellow eyes stared up at me as it meowed softly. It

was as if Mittons was welcoming me as I stepped closer.

The Book of Dreams

Everything else looked to be intact, including the window and green shower curtain, which was curled to one side.

"Did you find anything or anyone?" Amy called out.

I ducked my head out through the doorway and yelled,

"No, just the cat."

"Oh. It was probably Mittons just causing trouble. Come back, let's finish this movie."

Week 2

By the second week, strange things began to unfold. Aside from the strange crash, the kitchen window was found open every morning. We were both certain that the window was locked and closed the night before. The strange phenomenon forced us to do "surveillance checks" before going to bed. We even made a checklist:

The Book of Dreams

- Is the kitchen window closed and locked?

- Is the freezer and refrigerator door closed?

- Is the front door locked and closed?

- Are the other windows closed and locked?

Despite our efforts, we still found discrepancies during the second week. It all started on Wednesday night. We were on the couch, watching a movie called "Till Death Do Us Part." It was a great thriller, and we were enjoying it until something unexpected happened. We heard something fall and break. At first, we thought it was a sound from the movie, but then it happened again during a scene with no dialogue or sound. We looked at each other in fear.

"Did you hear that?" I asked Amy.

"Yeah," she replied weakly.

"What the hell was that? I think it came from the bathroom. Stay here; I'll check it out."

The Book of Dreams

Amy stayed on the couch, and I walked over to the bathroom, which was adjacent to the kitchen. The wooden floor creaked slightly beneath my footsteps. As I approached the bathroom, I saw light pouring from beneath the door. A shadow slowly passed as I stood in front of the door. I clutched the cold doorknob and pushed it down.

I entered and saw the cat sitting on top of the toilet seat. Its yellow eyes stared up at me as it meowed softly. Everything else looked intact, including the window and green shower curtain, which was curled to one side.

"Well, did you find anything or anyone?" Amy called out.

I ducked my head out through the doorway and yelled, "No, just the cat."

"Oh. It was probably Mittons just causing trouble. Come back; let's finish this movie."

The Book of Dreams

Week 3

By the third week, we were both not sleeping well. It became difficult to sleep there compared to two weeks ago. At night, we'd hear the sound of someone walking around the unit, despite there being no traces of anyone the next day. It was odd.

At first, we thought it was the cat, Mittons, who was walking around at night. But the footsteps were too heavy to be from a cat. Unfortunately, this strange phenomenon was happening. We didn't know or understand why. By Wednesday, things got really weird within the apartment.

"Did you leave the cabinets open last night?" Amy asked.

"No. Why? What happened now?"

"Come with me," she said.

The Book of Dreams

I followed her out of the bedroom, where I was working, and into the kitchen. There, we saw something really weird. The doors for the cabinets, pantry, and even the drawers were all open. It was as if someone was looking for something. Nothing was out of place, but the doors were left open.

"I didn't do this," I answered.

"Then who did, David? Who did?"

"I don't know. What is this, an interrogation? Why are you talking to me like this?"

"Like what?" she barked back.

"Like I'm some kind of criminal. I told you, I didn't do this!"

"Then who the hell did? The damn cat?"

Mittons meowed softly as he sat on the kitchen counter, watching us argue.

"Maybe? I don't know. I have to get back to work."

"Just go. Leave me alone then!" Amy hollered.

The Book of Dreams

I ignored her words and returned to the guest bedroom. My co-worker was shockingly staring at me because she could see I was feeling flustered. It was at that moment when I realized my microphone hadn't been muted; she had heard everything.

"Is everything okay?"

"Yeah. Sorry about that, Amanda. I'm apartment-sitting for my friend who is in Thailand right now. It's been a bit tense in here. I think we're just getting on each other's nerves."

Amanda smiled. "It's okay. Maybe the upcoming blizzard will help?"

I laughed. "How so?"

"Well, you know. Light a fire, pour some wine, and forget the time. That's what I always say," she said, winking at me.

The Book of Dreams

"You know, that's not a bad idea. But it's been difficult here."

"Why is that?"

I sighed. "You know. New place and all. It's an unfamiliar setting."

"Why not call your friend and check-in? That might help calm you both down, to hear his voice. When is he supposed to return?"

"Next week, Friday," I answered. "You know, that's not a bad idea. I think I will."

After work, I sat in the living room with Amy and called Travis. The ringing rattled through the phone's speaker as we stared at the screen with his name on it. His photo was of him and me in Mexico, in front of some ruins. The fireplace crackled, trying to mimic the real thing. "That's a nice photo of you," Amy commented.

"Thanks," I said.

The Book of Dreams

"Yeah?" the voice on the other end said.

"Travis? Is that you?"

"Oh yeah. Hey, bro, what's up? Sorry, I was just waking up.

I had a wild night. You wouldn't believe it!"

"Sorry, but Amy is here with me."

"Oh, sorry. Hey, Amy, how are you?"

"Fine," she flatly answered.

"What's up? Everything going alright over there?"

"Yeah. Well, it's been a little weird. There have been some

strange occurrences here."

"Oh? What kind of strange occurrences?"

"Well, you know, some weird things."

"Like what, David? What are you saying?"

"For one thing, your cat kind of freaks us out. He stares at

us a lot and meows softly."

The Book of Dreams

"Oh yeah. Mittons is a little weird in the winter. He misses being outside and humping stray cats," Travis said, chuckling.

"It's not just that. It's other things too, man. Like the cabinet doors have been open every morning, the kitchen window is open too, even though we make sure we lock it the night before."

"Oh yeah, I know why that's happening."

"Why is that?" I asked, looking at Amy.

Suddenly, the phone call abruptly ended.

"Travis? Crap! Are you there?"

I tried calling him again, but the call went straight to voicemail.

The Book of Dreams

Week 4

We were unable to get a hold of Travis after that.

Thankfully, this was the final week, and he was supposed

to return the day after tomorrow. Just two more days, I

thought as we laid in bed. Last night was rough. We

cooked some Thai cashew nut dish, and the fish sauce

really stunk up the apartment.

We wanted to open the windows, but the blizzard

that passed made it difficult since the locks were frozen

shut. Throughout the night, we heard the cabinet doors

slowly close and open. It was a bit annoying and left us

with another sleepless night. Our arguments had been

steady and over minor things. We stepped into the kitchen

together and saw everything amiss.

"Ugh! What the hell is this?" Amy asked as we stared at

the kitchen floor.

The Book of Dreams

"You know, I know this is going to sound like a stupid explanation, but maybe this is just the fault of cheap Ikea workmanship?"

Amy laughed more out of frustration. "Ikea? What does Ikea have to do with any of this?" She pointed at the floor as Mittons scurried by over the spilled box of Count Chocula cereal. Upon seeing the facial expression of Count Chocula, the two started laughing together.

"I forgot how adorable this guy was," she said while holding the box up.

"It's my favorite cereal, you know," I added.

Suddenly, the door behind us unlocked and slowly opened with a subtle creaking sound. We both looked over and saw footprints forming on the floor over the snow that had entered from outside. Then, without warning, the door slammed shut and locked. We looked at each other in petrified silence.

The Book of Dreams

Two days later, Travis returned.

"So, how was it? Do you want to stay again? Why does it smell like the ocean in here?"

"Sorry about that," I answered. "We cooked Thai food a few days ago, and the fish sauce smell has been lingering."

"Oh. Has the ghost been bothering you?"

"Ghost? Is that what was happening?"

"Yeah. His name is Henry."

"Well, the door did open two days ago, and we saw footprints of someone or something leaving."

Travis laughed. "Oh good. The fish smell must have driven him out. Someone in Thailand told me that's how you get rid of ghosts. I wanted him to leave since he wasn't paying rent. Ghosts usually haunt houses, so why would a ghost haunt a vacant apartment anyway? I was always asking him to pay rent. All he would do was... hey, is that Count Chocula? I love that cereal!

The Book of Dreams

STORY 11 — AUGUST 26 2026

The August afternoon sun bathed the city in its

warm rays. People filled the streets, savoring the last days

of summer as autumn loomed on the horizon. In a vibrant

city like Chicago, each sunlit day was an opportunity to

explore, and this particular Friday morning was no

exception. Some individuals were heading to their offices,

while others embarked on their usual morning routines —

The Book of Dreams

jogging, grabbing coffee, or engaging in yoga sessions at Grant Park.

As for me, I started my day by gazing out of my hotel room window. There was an inexplicable fascination in observing the locals navigate their city. Perhaps it was the curiosity of a tourist, pondering about their daily lives. My agenda included a visit to the renowned art museum and a leisurely lunch at the park beside the locally-dubbed "Bean."

Despite spending most of my life in the city, returning for a visit always felt special. The city's charm persisted, even amidst the familiarity and memories embedded in my mind. Chicago had an allure that captivated both newcomers and those who had known it for years.

Since it was my last day in town, I aimed to make the most of it by squeezing in as much as possible. In

The Book of Dreams

addition to exploring the museum, I had plans to treat myself to a delectable dessert from my favorite vegan bakery. Little did I know, none of these plans would come to fruition.

Stepping outside, I embarked on my adventure. Birds chirped in the leafy trees lining the streets as I headed towards the iconic Chicago River. The river was a sight to behold, particularly in March when it was dyed green for St. Patrick's Day. The towering skyscrapers reaching towards the sky added to the city's impressive vista.

Crossing the bridge over the Chicago River, I paused to take in the view. The Riverwalk was bustling with joggers and kayakers navigating the waters. It was quite the feat, considering the rumors of heavy pollution in the river.

The Book of Dreams

My rumbling stomach diverted my attention from the scenic views. I entered a café and grabbed a morning bagel. Exiting the café, I exchanged pleasantries with the security officer in the lobby.

"Nice morning, isn't it?" he cheerfully remarked.

"It certainly is," I responded.

"Headed to work?" he inquired.

"I'm actually visiting from out of town," I explained.

"Well, welcome then! I'm Officer Rooney. If you need anything, don't hesitate to ask."

Grinning after sipping my Earl Grey tea, I introduced myself, "Thank you, Officer Rooney. I'm Alex."

"Pleasure to meet you, Alex! I'm Michael," he replied.

"Michael Rooney, any relation to Ireland?"

"Indeed, I'm from Ireland!" Michael's eyes twinkled.

A seasoned gentleman, he appeared to be in his late sixties or early seventies.

The Book of Dreams

"I've been working in this building for forty years. Today marks my retirement," he revealed.

"Congratulations, Michael!"

He chuckled heartily. "Thanks, Alex. By the way, have you been to the top of the building? I could take you up there for a quick view."

I hesitated. "I haven't, but I don't want to get you into trouble."

"Trouble? Son, I am trouble," he laughed. "I'm the supervisor, and it's my last day. I wanted a final view of this beautiful city."

"Thanks, Michael."

"Pleasure's mine. I'm celebrating tonight, you know."

"Oh?"

"I've got a corned beef with cabbage and potatoes in the slow cooker at home. Going to have a grand feast."

I chuckled. "Sounds like a delightful evening ahead."

The Book of Dreams

"Where are you from, Alex?"

"Florida," I replied.

"Ah, Florida! You folks have it made down there. None of this snow business like we have here."

As we reached the rooftop entrance, Michael sifted through a jumble of keys.

"We're near the lunch area. Let me know if you want a soda," he offered.

"No, thank you. I've got my tea," I said, holding up my tea cup.

"You young people and your tea," he remarked with a grin.

"I'm a coffee man myself, first thing in the morning."

"Black or with cream?"

Michael gave me a sly smile. "Just like my women: sweet, rich, and black."

His unexpected innuendo caught me off guard, but I managed, "Are you married?"

The Book of Dreams

"I was. My wife, Kimmy, passed away a few years ago," he answered, his tone subdued.

As we arrived at the roof entrance, Michael located the right key.

"Watch your step," he advised.

We climbed a few steps and emerged onto the rooftop. A gust of wind greeted us, tousling his thin white hair as I clung to my tea and leftover bagel.

"Here we are," Michael announced.

The panoramic view was breathtaking. Skyscrapers surrounded us, and below, the "L" train crossed the bridges. Seagulls glided overhead, heading towards the lakefront.

"Something else, isn't it?" Michael marveled. "I'll miss this."

"Yeah, it truly is."

The Book of Dreams

"Look there!" Michael gestured excitedly. "The 'L' train, and over there, one of the bridges. It's always incredible to see human ingenuity."

Standing by his side, I followed his pointing finger.

"That's right. It's a busy morning," I commented as I observed the bustling bridges.

Then, the unexpected happened. A series of deafening rumbles shook the ground, and explosions erupted from the bridges in front of us.

"What's happening?" I exclaimed.

Before we could react, more explosions echoed, and the bridges crumbled into pieces. The watchtower structures collapsed, sending shockwaves through the city.

"What on earth?" I mumbled.

Michael clutched his chest, and a look of pain washed over his face.

"My heart... Alex, it hurts."

The Book of Dreams

Fear gripped me as I struggled to comprehend the situation. I reached for my phone, intending to call for help, but Michael's frail hand grabbed my jacket.

"No need. They need help down there," he said, gesturing towards the chaos below. "My time's come. Go, help them. Save as many as you can."

"No, Michael, we can get you help!" I protested.

He smiled gently. "You've already helped me, my boy. You gave me a moment I'll cherish, in this life and the next. It was nice to talk to you. In forty years, I've never had a conversation like this. I'm glad to call you a friend. Now go, help and save as many as you can."

Tears welled in my eyes as Michael closed his. His breathing slowed, and he passed away peacefully before me. Heartbroken, I fulfilled my promise, saving as many lives as I could amidst the chaos.

The Book of Dreams